The Child's World of
CARING

Library of Congress Cataloging in Publication Data

Moncure, Jane Belk.
Caring / Jane Belk Moncure.
p.   cm.
Originally published: c1980.
Summary: Simple text and scenes depict caring behavior, such as feeding
the wild birds all winter long, picking up paper and trash left by someone
else, teaching a friend to turn a cartwheel, and picking up your toys without
being asked.
ISBN 1-56766-297-8 (hardcover)
1. Caring in children—Juvenile literature.   2. Helping behavior in
children—Juvenile literature.   [1. Caring.]
I. Title.
BF723.C25M66   1996
177'.7—dc20   96-11838
                                CIP
                                AC

The Child's World of
CARING

By Jane Belk Moncure • Illustrated by Mechelle Ann

THE CHILD'S WORLD

4

What is caring?

When you hold your little brother on your shoulders so he can pick apples too—that's caring.

8

When you help a turtle across a path in the park so he will be safe—that's caring.

Caring is when you pick up paper and trash someone else left under the picnic table. Caring is putting the trash where it belongs.

When you leave wild flowers to bloom along a mountain trail so others can enjoy them too—that's caring.

When you put your brother's bicycle in the garage so it won't get wet or stolen—that's caring.

16

Caring is when you teach a friend how to turn a cartwheel.

18

And caring is wrapping your coat around a friend on a chilly day.

When you keep your toys picked up without being asked again and again—that's caring.

Caring is helping your dad plant a new tree after a storm knocked down the old one.

When you get a bandage for a friend who scraped her knee—that's caring.

When you feed and brush your puppy and give him clean water every day—that's caring.

Caring is when you listen to your parents and try to do the things they ask you to do. They ask because they care.

Can you think of other ways to show caring?